Mr. Brush
(The brush seller)

Anna, Mrs. Luigi, Mr. Luigi, Alex, and **Roberta**
(Mrs. Luigi makes pizza; Mr. Luigi makes ice cream.)

Noah
(The tropical fisherman)

Mrs. Pankhurst
(and Henrietta)

This is Migloo.

And this is the story
of Migloo's day.

Benny
(He doesn't do much.)

Roshan
(The traffic policeman)

Molly
(She makes orange juice.)

Juan and **Conchita**
(He goes down manholes;
she goes up telephone poles.)

Lottie and **Noggin** and **Kitty** and **Toto**
(Noggin thinks he's a Viking, and Kitty thinks she's a cat.)

Flossy
(The cotton-candy seller)

Boris
(He puts up posters.)

Basil
(He sells doughnuts.)

Mia
(She puts up antennas.)

Charlie
(The newspaper man)

Dr. Whom
(She is Sunnytown's doctor.)

Dougal
(He drives the forklift.)

Farmer Tom and **Suki**
(From Sunnytown Farm)

Terry and **Bea** and **Lizzy**
(Terry and Bea run Sunnytown's taxi service.)

Miss Othmar
(She is a teacher.)

Polly
(She works at the factory.)

William Bee

Gwendolyn and **Cecily**
(Or is it the other way around?)

Eric and **Ernie**
(Brother builders)

Sebastian
(He works at the factory.)

Mr. Tompion
(The clock winder)

Zebedee
(The costume-shop man)

"The Great Fernando"
(and Milo the Monkey)

Zoë
(She works at the factory.)

Harry and **Alphonso**
(The Sunnytown firefighters)

Freda and **Bobby** and **Olivia** and **Bert**
(From the Sunnytown garage)

François and **Agatha**
(They deliver the mail.)

Mr. McGregor and **Rose**
(They grow lots of plants.)

Mr. and **Mrs. Smudge** and **Scruff**
(The messiest family in town)

Isabella
(The traffic guard)

Reg
(He sells fruit and veggies.)

Otto
(He's always around.)

Indira
and **Flopsy** and **Tiny Mouse**

Mr. and **Mrs. Dickens**
(He sells books, and she teaches with them.)

Lenny
(He sweeps up.)

Sydney and **Lily** and **Florence**
Sydney is the window washer, and Florence bakes bread.)

Dylan
(The school caretaker)

Daisy and **Felix** and **Amit**
(They make sandwiches and sell carpets.)

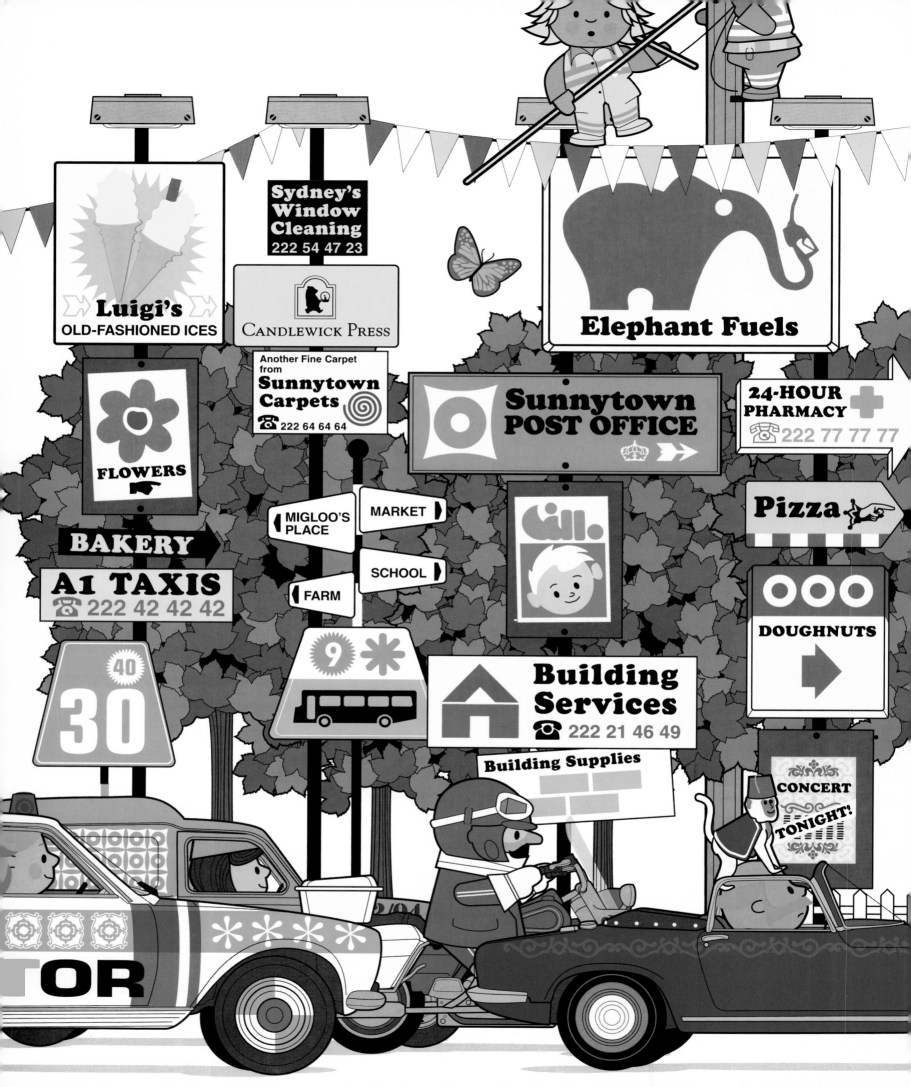

Migloo's Day

william bee

Sunnytown
Sister city: Sillycone Valley

Migloo's up nice and early this morning, and he's feeling quite hungry.

"You look like you're ready for breakfast, Migloo!" says Farmer Tom. "I'm off to the market. Why don't you hop on?"
Migloo wags his tail, which means "Yes, please!"

With special thanks to:
art director **Audrey Keri-Nagy** and editor **Maria Tunney**.
Also to: **Jane Winterbotham**, **Deirdre McDermott**, **Alice Blacker**, **Sue Tarsky**, and **Jodie Hodges**.

AT THE MARKET

Migloo thanks Farmer Tom with a wag of his tail, and then he sets off to explore the market. It's full of people selling all sorts of things—brushes, flowers, china cats—and—mmmm—there are lots and lots of delicious smells!

BOOKS

CARPETS

POST OFFICE
FIRE STATION
SCHOOL
FARM

? QUESTION TIME ?
Can you see Migloo?
Where's the butterfly?
Can you find the pink knitting?

Building Services
☎ 222 21 46 49

CONCERT TONIGHT

9 *

FRUIT and VEGETABLES

GREEN THUMB

AT THE TOWN SQUARE

Migloo can smell Molly's ripe, zingy oranges and Florence's just-baked crusty bread. He can also smell his FAVORITE smell of all: Suki's super sizzling sausages! But can Migloo find them?

? QUESTION TIME ?

Where's Tiny Mouse?
Who's on a ladder?
Who has lost a shoe?
Has Henrietta laid an egg?

Oh, yes! Migloo certainly has a good nose—especially
for sausages!
"Hello, Migloo! I've made these just for you," says Suki.
Migloo wags his tail, ever such a lot,
which means "Thank you, Suki.
I do love sausages—
ever such a lot!'

After all that breakfast, Migloo
would like something sweet.

"One of my famous Knickerbocker Glories!" says Mr. Luigi.
Migloo is delighted! He wags his tail, which, of course,
means "Thank you, Mr. Luigi. This is the best
Knickerbocker Glory EVER!"

Who has Migloo spotted now? It's Zebedee! His costume shop has all sorts of fancy dresses and fancy suits, and fancy hats and fancy boots. Migloo likes trying on hats. This one has a big feather on it—PIRATE MIGLOO!

What a great start to Migloo's day! And now Sydney offers Migloo a ride in his sidecar.

"Jump in, Migloo," says Sydney. "I'm off to the Sunnytown Factory. It's got a LOT of dirty windows."

Migloo wags his tail, which means "Great!"

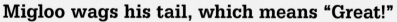

AT THE SUNNYTOWN FACTORY

Migloo and Sydney arrive at the factory—
it's a very busy place! It's noisy, too!
There are big, noisy machines and big,
noisy trucks and a big, noisy forklift.
So will Migloo be able to hear the bell that
means "IT'S LUNCHTIME"?

factory shop

QUESTION TIME

Can you see a bell?
Who has swapped hats?
Can you find Cecily?
Who is reading?

SUNNYTOWN NEWS
RUBBER DUCKS MAKE BID FOR FREEDOM!
READ ALL ABOUT IT!

PIZZA

Oh, yes! Migloo's ears are almost as good
as his nose. Daisy makes sandwiches
for everyone at the factory.
"And I've got one extra for my little
friend Migloo," she says.

Daisy and Migloo take
some sandwiches over to Dougal,
the forklift driver.

"Tomato and lettuce? Mmmm,
my favorite," says Dougal.
Migloo wags his tail,
which means "Mine too!"

Next door is the builders' yard.
Eric is stacking tiles in his wheelbarrow.
"Hi, Migloo. Can you sit on top so they don't slip off?"
Migloo wags his tail, which means "Certainly, as
long as I can wear a hard hat
in case *I* slip off."

François has just picked up a mysterious package from
Polly at the factory and spots
Migloo in his hard hat.
"That hat looks perfect for
a motorbike ride! Jump on,
Migloo, and hold on tight!"

AT THE FIRE STATION

Migloo jumps down from the motorbike and picks up the scent of something JAMMY and DOUGHY and NUTTY. What could it be? Migloo heads in the direction of the fire station. There he finds his friends Harry and Alphonso and—aha!—delicious jam doughnuts!

"How about a nice cup of tea, Migloo?" asks Alphonso. Migloo wags his tail, which means "Yes please— if it comes with a nice jam doughnut!"

After tea and doughnuts, Migloo helps Roshan and Isabella load road signs into the police jeep. The signs are very bossy: STOP! GO LEFT! GO RIGHT! YIELD! GIVE UP!

Behind the police station, Roshan shows Migloo what happens when drivers fail to: STOP! GO LEFT! GO RIGHT! YIELD! GIVE UP!

Roshan asks Migloo if he would like to come for a ride.
Migloo wags his tail, which means "Yes, PLEASE
Mr. Policeman, SIR!"

AT SUNNYTOWN SCHOOL

How exciting! Roshan and Isabella are visiting the school for "Don't Fall Off Your Bike Week." Migloo is very eager to help. But first he MUST visit Mrs. Luigi's café. She always has a special snack just for Migloo, and today it's a slice of her homemade pepperoni pizza!

? QUESTION TIME ?
Who's holding a balloon?
Who has some doughnuts?
Where's Little White Owl?

After eating his pizza, Migloo helps Roshan and Isabella with the bike safety lesson. It's dangerous work— the new cones that François brought from the Sunnytown Factory are all getting BUMPED!

Here is Lily, bumping into a cone.

Here is Alex, bumping into a cone.

And here are Lottie and Anna, bumping into each other.

Migloo decides it's safer indoors, where the
children in the art class are making fancy hats.
Felix has made a hat for Migloo, and Migloo is very
pleased with it—KING MIGLOO!

The bell rings for the end of school, but today
the children are going somewhere special.
Miss Othmar and Mrs. Dickens invite
Migloo to come, too.
Migloo wags his tail, which means
"That would be nice—as long as I
can wear my hat."

AT THE GARAGE

They've stopped at the garage.
There's something wrong with the school bus!
The engine is smoking, and oil is running out
from underneath.
"OH, NO!" cry the children. Migloo rushes off
to find Bert, the chief mechanic.

"Hello, Migloo," says Bert.

Migloo runs around Bert, barking and wagging his tail, which means "The school bus has broken down, and all the children are very upset!"

"Look at all that SMOKE, Bert! Can you fix it?" asks Miss Othmar.

Bert puts the bus up on the lift and pokes around with his wrench.

"Oh, dear. It looks like your motor has jammed! It will take AGES to fix."

No one knows what to do!
But Migloo—who has had a lovely day being driven around by his friends and being fed sausages, ice cream, sandwiches, and pizza—suddenly has an idea!

GOODNESS! LOOK! Everyone's come to the rescue!
But where could they all be going?

Migloo runs back to all his friends, wagging his tail, which, of course, means

"The school bus has broken down! The children need your help!"

AT SUNNYTOWN PARK

Time for the concert! With a front-row seat for Migloo! He settles down to listen to the music and wags his tail, which means either "It's great that all my friends were able to help the children get to their concert and play their instruments!" or "What I'd really like right now . . . is a nice plate of French fries!"

William Bee's Busy Page

Sunnytown is such a busy place. There's always so much going on! There are lots and lots of people working, eating, driving, and playing—which means there are lots and lots of things for YOU to look for!

Who's in the tree?

Whose hat is that?

What's wrong with Migloo?

ANSWERS: 1. No eyebrows! 2. Five legs! 3. Extra eyebrows! 4. "Where's my tail?" 5. Missing patch!

ANSWERS:
Gwendolyn
Milo the Monkey
Gray Squirrel
Crab
Little White Owl
Flopsy

ANSWERS:
Cecily
Tiny Mouse
Penguin
Red Squirrel
Parrot
Indira

ANSWERS: 1. Agatha, the mail carrier 2. Noggin, the Viking 3. Dylan, the school caretaker 4. Benny, who DOESN'T sweep up! 5. François, the mail carrier 6. Reg, the greengrocer 7. Mr. McGregor, the gardener 8. Suki, the sausage seller 9. Sydney, the window washer 10. Lenny, who DOES sweep up!

1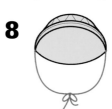
2
3
4
5
6
7
8
9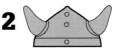
10

Can you spot ALL 29 red elephant piggy banks (including this one)?

Kitty's china cats pop up everywhere! William Bee found 32 (including this one)—can you?

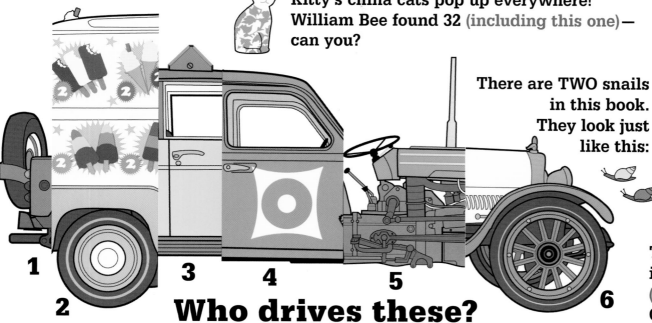

There are TWO snails in this book. They look just like this:

There are 27 soccer balls in this book (not including this one). Can you find them all?

Who drives these?

ANSWERS: 1. Roshan, the traffic policeman 2. Mr. Luigi, the ice-cream seller 3. Terry, the taxi driver 4. Agatha, the mail carrier 5. Farmer Tom 6. William Bee

What are we looking at here?

1. At the Garage

2. At Sunnytown Park

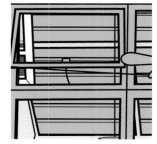
3. At Sunnytown School

4. At the Fire Station

5. At the Market

ANSWERS: 1. That's Mrs. Smudge's car. She's getting gas at the garage. Harry and Alphonso are on the fire truck's ladder. 3. A squirrel's tail? It's Gray Squirrel, running across the roof of the school. 4. Well, you can find Amit, the carpet seller, all over the place but you can just see Polly having a banana. 5. That's Reg's fruit and vegetable truck.

Who carries these?

1

2

3

5

4

6

7

8

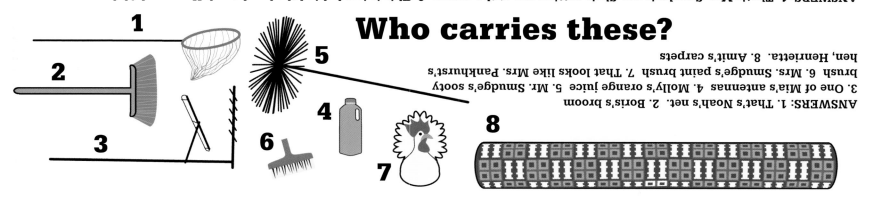

ANSWERS: 1. That's Noah's net. 2. Boris's broom
3. One of Mia's antennas 4. Molly's orange juice 5. Mr. Smudge's sooty brush 6. Mrs. Smudge's paint brush 7. That looks like Mrs. Pankhurst's hen, Henrietta. 8. Amit's carpets

Who do these legs belong to?

1

2

3

4

5

6

ANSWERS: 1. Basil 2. Rose 3. Reg 4. Agatha 5. Lenny 6. Indira

What are these?

ANSWERS: The blue symbol is for the traffic police. The red one is for the fire department. And the green one is for the ambulance.

Whose bike is this?

ANSWER: It belongs to Mr. Smudge, the chimney sweep. At the concert, his brushes are leaning against it.

On the pages where you see William Bee holding his yellow QUESTION TIME sign, it means there are LOTS of things to find!

And if you feel like getting even BUSIER, you can find the answers to ALL the questions he asks below on EACH of the 8 pages where his yellow QUESTION TIME sign appears!

So, that means you can find Flopsy 8 times and missing shoes in 8 different places! And lots of people eating bananas and wearing glasses! Phew . . . that IS busy!

Busy Bee Questions

Here are all the things to find and how many times to find them in total!

Who's reading? (13) Who's on a ladder? (24) Who has lost a shoe? (9) Has Henrietta laid an egg? (8) Who's holding an ice cream or candy? (21) And who's DROPPED an ice cream? (2) Who's wearing glasses? (68) Who's holding a balloon? (8) Who has some doughnuts? (26) CAN YOU SEE: Migloo? (8) Butterfly? (8) Tiny Mouse? (8) A bell? (9) The pink knitting? (10) Cecily and Gwendolyn? (8 each) Indira? (8) Red Squirrel and Gray Squirrel? (8 each) Little White Owl? (8) Penguin? (8) Mr. Smudge—usually just his sooty brush? (8) Milo the Monkey? (8) Flopsy? (8) An umbrella? (9) Parrot? (8) Who has swapped hats? (10 pairs) Who's eating a banana? (15) AND . . . What's Crab holding? (8)

Good-bye, Migloo.

See you again soon.

 First U.S. edition 2015. Library of Congress Catalog Card Number 2013957312. ISBN 978-0-7636-7374-1. This book was typeset in URW Egyptienne. The illustrations were created digitally. Candlewick Press, 99 Dover Street, Somerville, Massachusetts 02144. visit us at www.candlewick.com. Printed in Shenzhen, Guangdong, China. 15 16 17 18 19 20 CCP 10 9 8 7 6 5 4 3 2 1